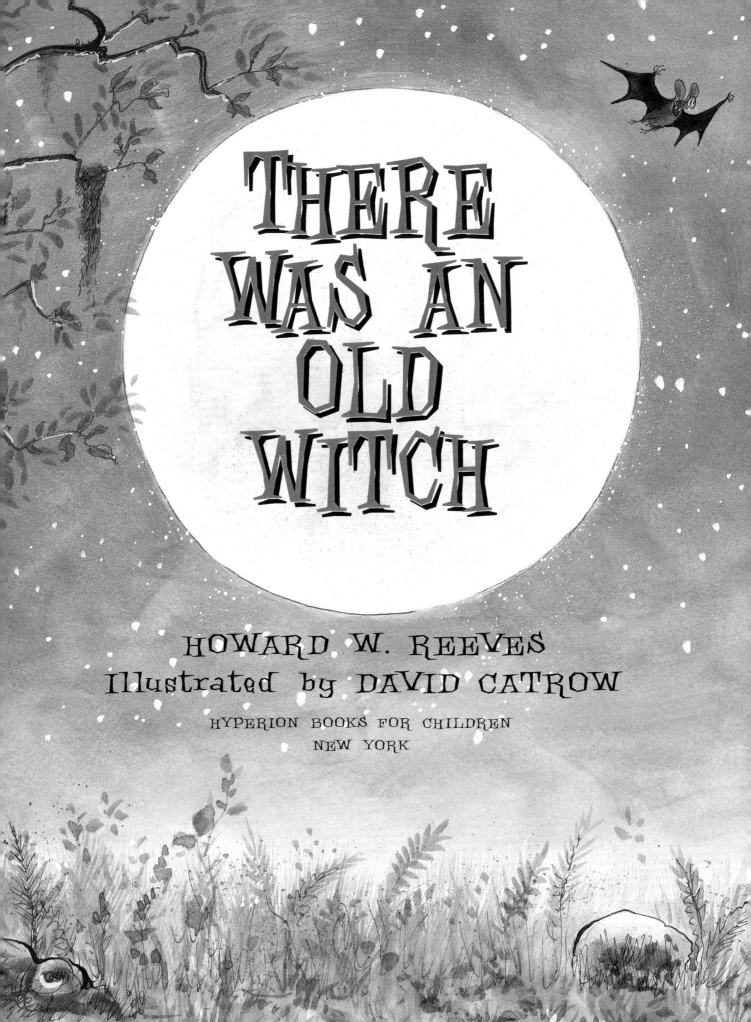

THERE WAS AN OLD WITCH

HOWARD W. REEVES
Illustrated by DAVID CATROW

HYPERION BOOKS FOR CHILDREN
NEW YORK

There was an old witch
who wanted a bat.
I know why
she wanted the bat.
But I won't tell you that.

There was an old witch
who captured a cat
that once in her lap
scratched, scritched, and spat.
She captured the cat
to bag the bat.
I know why
she wanted the bat.
　　　But I won't tell you that.

ON

OFF

There was an old witch
who created a creature
whose howling and yowling
was its finest feature.
She created the creature
to catch the cat
that once in her lap
scratched, scritched, and spat.
She captured the cat
to bag the bat.
I know why
she wanted the bat.
But I won't tell you that.

There was an old witch
who unearthed a mummy
who because of its wrappings
was a little bit bumbly.
She unearthed the mummy
to catch the creature.
She created the creature
to catch the cat
that once in her lap
scratched, scritched, and spat.
She captured the cat
to bag the bat.
I know why
she wanted the bat.
But I won't tell you that.

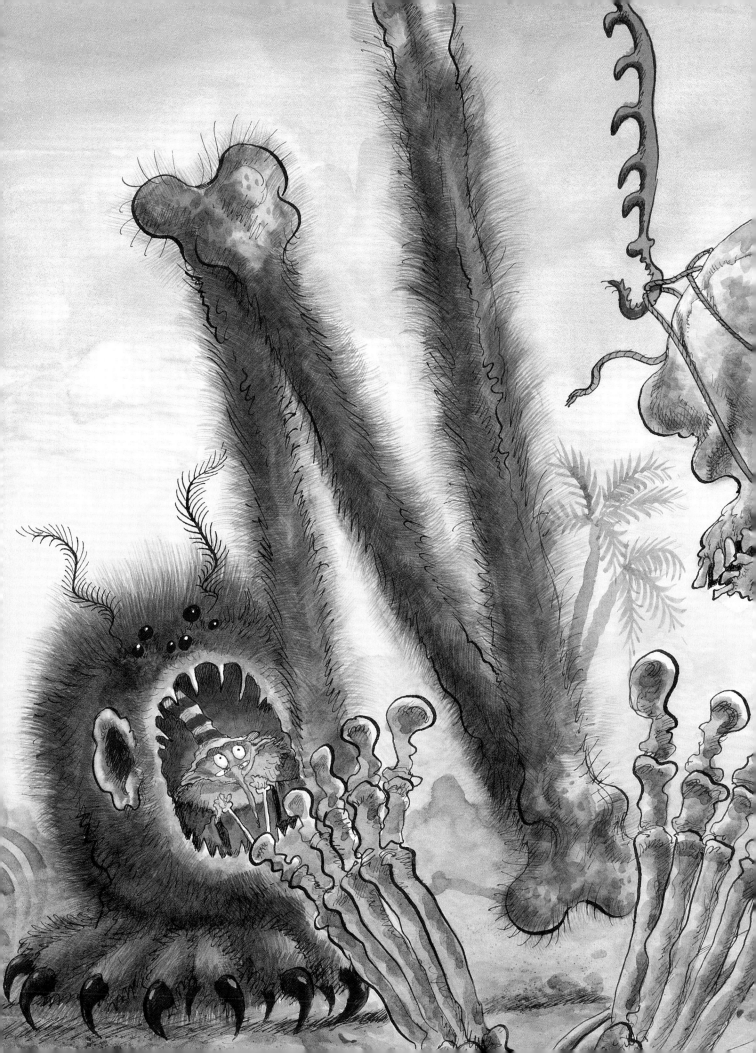

There was an old witch
who assembled a skel'ton
who rattled his bones
with moans and groans.
She assembled the skel'ton
to catch the mummy.
She unearthed the mummy
to catch the creature.
She created the creature
to catch the cat
that once in her lap
scratched, scritched, and spat.
She captured the cat
to bag the bat.
I know why
she wanted the bat.
        But I won't tell you that.

There was an old witch
who conjured a haunt
that aaaahhhhed and oooohed
its wails and taunts.
She conjured the haunt
to catch the skel'ton.
She assembled the skel'ton
to catch the mummy.
She unearthed the mummy
to catch the creature.
She created the creature
to catch the cat
that once in her lap
scratched, scritched, and spat.
She captured the cat
to bag the bat.

And why, oh why,
did she want a bat?
To gobble up a pesky gnat?
To carry off a sniveling brat?
To befriend her lonesome rat?

No—
Nothing more
than to adorn
her Halloween hat!
　　And that's that.